Charles Emerson Beecher

Brachiospongidae

A memoir on a group of silurian sponges

Charles Emerson Beecher

Brachiospongidae
A memoir on a group of silurian sponges

ISBN/EAN: 9783742839718

Manufactured in Europe, USA, Canada, Australia, Japa

Cover: Foto ©Andreas Hilbeck / pixelio.de

Manufactured and distributed by brebook publishing software
(www.brebook.com)

Charles Emerson Beecher

Brachiospongidae

MEMOIRS OF THE PEABODY MUSEUM OF YALE UNIVERSITY.
VOL. II, PART I.

BRACHIOSPONGIDÆ:

A

MEMOIR

ON A

GROUP OF SILURIAN SPONGES.

WITH SIX PLATES.

BY

CHARLES EMERSON BEECHER.

NEW HAVEN, CONN.:
PRINTED FOR THE MUSEUM.
1889.

MEMOIRS OF THE PEABODY MUSEUM OF YALE UNIVERSITY.
VOL. II, PART I.

BRACHIOSPONGIDÆ:

A

MEMOIR

ON A

GROUP OF SILURIAN SPONGES.

WITH SIX PLATES.

BY

CHARLES EMERSON BEECHER.

NEW HAVEN, CONN.:
PRINTED FOR THE MUSEUM.
1889.

BRACHIOSPONGIDÆ.

(With Six Plates.)

By Charles Emerson Beecher.

BRACHIOSPONGIA, Marsh.

These sponges were made known as early as 1838, and were the first strictly American paleozoic sponges described. The systematic position of Brachiospongia, however, has remained hitherto undetermined. Professor Karl A. von Zittel placed the genus provisionally in the family Euretidæ, Zittel, under the order Hexactinellida. This arrangement was followed by Dr. G. J. Hinde, although he regarded the position of the genus uncertain, as its structure was unknown.

The basis of our information of these variable, and often imperfectly preserved fossils must rest largely upon the results of the study of more recent forms, and the interpretation of the fossil must be in the same terms used for the living organism.

The first systematic grouping of sponges, based upon reliable characters, was worked out with great care, in Zittel's memoirs, published during the years 1876–78. All subsequent writers have accepted the principles which he established, and have adopted his main subdivisions.

The later investigations of Dr. G. J. Hinde have largely supplemented our knowledge of the fossil forms, and with the crowning work by Dr. F. E. Schulze,[1] on the recent species of the order Hexactinellida, the paleontologist can readily interpret his observations, and classify the various species and genera which preserve the main features of their structure.

HISTORICAL ACCOUNT OF BRACHIOSPONGIA.

1838.

G. TROOST. Description d'un Nouveau Genre de Fossiles. (Mém. Soc. Géol. France, Vol. III, pp. 95, 96; Pl. XI, figs. 8, 9, 10.)

The new genus described in this paper was a cephalopod (Conotubularia), which has since been considered as a synonym under the genus Orthoceras. A new species of Asaphus (*A. megalopthalmus*) is also indicated and figured. The paper concludes with "Description d'un fossile représenté dans la pl. XI, fig. 8, 9, 10," where an account is given of a fossil which is at once recognized as BRACHIOSPONGIA. The specimen has nine arms, and is described as silicified. Dr. Troost suggests its affinities with sponges, and states that he discovered the fossil in a limestone occurring in Davidson County, Tennessee. Singularly, no name was proposed, and apparently, no notice has been taken of the description and figures in any publication, previous to Dr. G. J. Hinde's Catalogue of the Fossil Sponges in the British Museum, 1883.

It seems more than probable that the specimen in the possession of Dr. Troost, in 1838, and described by him, is identical with the one which was made the type of *Brachiospongia reuierrana*, by Professor O. C. Marsh, in 1867, and is now illustrated on Plate I of the present memoir. The evidence is based upon the striking resemblance between this example and the figures on Plate XI of Troost's paper. The general dimensions agree very closely, and in addition, the diameters and height of the neck, and the length of the longest arm are the same. Besides having a like number of arms, and agreeing in size, a more marked

[1] Report on the Hexactinellida collected by H. M. S. Challenger during the years 1873-1876. Zoölogy, vol. xxi, 1887.

resemblance may be traced, if the type of *B. romerana* is placed in a slightly inclined position, which is the one naturally assumed on account of the imperfection of the lower portion, and the arms then compared seriatim in respect to direction, length, and size. It must be assumed, however, that the lithograph was made without reversing the drawings, and that the specimen appears reversed on the plate. The inference is supported by the fact that the shadows on all the figures are manifestly on the wrong side.

A comparison under these conditions shows that the widest divergence between any two arms is adjacent to the longest and unbroken one. The latter arm is oblique to the longitudinal diameter of the osculum, and the three shortest broken arms are adjacent to it, and are situated on the side opposite the greatest interbrachial space. The side view offers similar points for comparison, if the specimen is placed in the proper position. It should also be noted, that this individual shows a greater elevation of the neck, and of the arms near their origin, than has been observed in any other.

The history of the type specimen is somewhat obscure, but nevertheless furnishes additional proof in support of its identity with the one described by Troost. According to the best evidence at present attainable, it was in the possession of Dr. Yandell in 1855, who at that time was custodian of a portion, at least, of the Troost collection. Rev. H. C. Hovey obtained the specimen in exchange, and subsequently transferred it to Professor O. C. Marsh, who, after describing it in 1867, presented it to the Museum of Yale College.

1858.

D. D. OWEN. Kentucky Geological Survey, Vol. II, p. 111.

In his report on the geology of Franklin County, Owen refers to the principal external features of these sponges, and proposes for them the specific name *digitata*, which he places under the genus *Scyphia*, Oken. The locality of their occurrence is described, and the geological horizon is referred to a position near the middle of a detailed section of Lower Silurian strata, at Frankfort, Ky.

1862.

R. OWEN.   Indiana Geological Survey, 1859–60, pp. 362, 363, fig. 1.

A very imperfect specimen is figured, accompanied by a brief description, in which the name is changed to *Syphonia digitata.*   In a letter written to Professor Marsh, in 1867, Professor Owen states that the alteration in the name was through inadvertence.

1865.

H. A. WARD.   Eighteenth Annual Report New York State Cabinet of Natural History, p. 29, fig. 4.

A wood-cut of an eleven-armed specimen is given, and referred to "Amorphozonm?"   The same figure is reproduced by Professor Ward, under the name "Amorphospongia ——," in his "Catalogue of Casts of Fossils," published in 1866.   This specimen was made the type of *Brachiospongia lyoni*, by Professor Marsh in 1867.

1867.

O. C. MARSH.   American Journal of Science, 2d Series, Vol. XLIV, p. 88.

In this preliminary paper, the genus BRACHIOSPONGIA is first proposed and described, and the species *B. remerana* and *B. lyoni* are named provisionally.   *B. remerana* was proposed for a nine-armed specimen which now appears to be the original type of Troost's description and figures.   The name *B. lyoni* was given to a specimen having eleven rays, then in the collection of S. S. Lyon.   Photographs and lithographic figures of the type specimen *B. remerana* were made at this time, but copies of the former alone were distributed.

1868.

O. C. MARSH.   Proceedings of the American Association for the Advancement of Science, p. 160.

A paper was read at the sixteenth meeting of the Association, held at Burlington, Vt., "On some new Fossil Sponges from the Lower Silurian." In the published volume of the proceedings, the title only of this paper appears.

1874.

H. C. Hovey. Transactions Kansas Academy of Science, pp. 344, 345, figs. 1, 2. Republished in the Scientific American, pp. 387, 388, figs. 1, 2, June, 1875.

An incomplete historical review is presented of the published notices of BRACHIOSPONGIA, beginning with the account by D. D. Owen, in 1858. A wood-cut of the type of *B. ramerana*, made from one of the photographs distributed by Professor Marsh, and a figure of a specimen referred to *B. hoveyi* (Marsh), first appear in this publication. The name *B. hoveyi* was proposed for an example with twelve arms, and was announced in the paper read by Professor Marsh, before the American Association. The specimen figured, which was not the type, is an abnormal individual of *B. digitata*, in which the arms have been developed spirally about the axis. A strict enumeration of the partially and fully grown arms indicates fifteen as the number, but the neck is imperfect, and there were probably more in the entire specimen.

Subsequent notices of these fossils are mainly of the character of references, and include the following:

1877.

Joseph LeConte. Elements of Geology, p. 302, fig. 290. (*B. ramerana.*)

S. A. Miller. The American Palæozoic Fossils, p. 42. (*B. digitata, B. lyoni, B. ramerana.*)

1878.

K. A. Zittel. Handbuch der Palæontologie, Band 1, p. 173. (*Brachiospongia.*)

1880.

F. Rœmer. Lethæa Geognostica, 1 Th., p. 319, fig. 61. (*B. ramerana.*)

1883.

G. J. Hinde. Catalogue of the Fossil Sponges in the Geological Department of the British Museum, p. 102. (*B. digitata = B. ramerana* and *B. lyoni.*)

ACKNOWLEDGMENTS.

The abundance and richness of the material which has been placed at my disposal is due to the long continued efforts of Professor O. C. Marsh, who for several years secured all the specimens found at the principal locality. It was the original intention of Professor Marsh to publish a memoir upon the genus BRACHIOSPONGIA, as soon as the completeness of the material should warrant it; but the development of his researches in the fossil vertebrate fields of the Western States and Territories soon reached such proportions, and became so important, as to preclude the carrying out of his original purpose. The publication of this memoir in its present form is also due to the kind liberality of Professor Marsh.

I wish to express my obligation to Mr. Moritz Fischer, of the Kentucky Geological Survey, for the privilege of examining and figuring a fine twelve-armed specimen belonging to the State Museum, and, also, for courtesies shown me during a recent visit to the region where these fossils have been obtained.

The collections have been considerably enriched through the efforts of Mr. E. C. Went, of Frankfort, Ky., in the discovery of a new locality yielding a number of interesting examples occurring *in situ*, and furnishing the first definite knowledge as to their true position in the geological series.

Rev. H. C. Hovey, of Bridgeport, Conn., has kindly given me an opportunity to study several specimens in his cabinet, and has communicated important historical points. He first systematically collected BRACHIOSPONGIA, and observed the geographical distribution of the genus. A number of the specimens in the Yale University Museum were obtained through his researches.

GEOLOGICAL POSITION.

The precise horizon of the strata furnishing BRACHIOSPONGIA has been uncertain. Hitherto, all writers have agreed in referring them to the Silurian, the particular beds being unknown. Rev. H. C. Hovey placed them in the Birdseye limestone.[1] None of the specimens, however, present any

---

Trans. Kansas Acad. Sci., p. 344, 1874.

evidence of having come from that horizon, and all the known localities furnishing BRACHIOSPONGIA are at some distance from exposures of the Birdseye, and at a much higher level. A single example was found in a loose piece of rock, by Mr. Moritz Fischer, at Benson Station, Franklin County, which was apparently derived from strata belonging to the middle of the Trenton series. So far as known, this is the lowest horizon at which these fossils have been observed. At the famous locality on Benson Creek, about three miles above Benson Station, where nearly all the specimens first discovered were obtained, no accurate determination of their position could be made, as they were found loose in the debris on the hillsides, and on the banks and bed of the creek. The same observations apply to the locality near Bridgeport, Franklin County. At Cedar Run, in an exposure discovered by Mr. E. C. Went, of Frankfort, BRACHIOSPONGIA is found in place, and its true horizon and associated fossils have been determined.

The beds consist of a fine cherty nodular limestone lying above the horizon of *Orthis borealis*, which has been considered as the upper member of the Trenton. They are succeeded by the lower beds of the Hudson group with their abundant and characteristic fossils. The adjacent limestones are without beds of chert, and are coarser grained, so that the rocks containing BRACHIOSPONGIA are easily recognized.

With this information, the sponge horizon was traced over a considerable extent of territory, and connected with the other localities at which BRACHIOSPONGIA occurs. It was found that with the exception of the single specimen from the Middle Trenton, at Benson Station, all the localities in Franklin County were at the same horizon. Similar beds cap the Trenton at Lexington, Ky.

Under the description of *B. digitata*, mention is made of a specimen from the Middle Hudson of Spencer County, Ky., which presents several points of difference from the ordinary form, both in its general characters, and condition of preservation. As a whole, however, this species has a comparatively limited vertical range, and its occurrence is of geological importance.

3

On account of the faunal and lithological similarity between the Trenton and Hudson groups in central Kentucky, the horizon of *B. digitata*, taken in connection with the character of the rock and associated fossils, is an important one, as furnishing a definite and easily recognizable bed separating the two formations. The Utica Slate is absent in this region, and without more precise information, it may be desirable to correlate with it the Brachiosponge beds, in which case the latter would represent a synchronous deposit, although physically different, from its sedimentation in deeper waters, probably at some distance from the shore line.

Associated Fossils.

Under the microscope, the rock is seen to be composed of the finely comminuted testaceous remains of crustacea and mollusca, mingled with some argillaceous and silicious material.

In general, the beds are nearly barren of fossils, and close scrutiny reveals but a meager fauna. The species which have been observed are given in the following list :

1. Brachiospongia digitata, *Owen.*   Rare.
2. Strobilospongia aurita, *Beecher.*   Rare.
3. ? Strobilospongia tuberosa, *Beecher.*   Rare.
4. Root tufts (basalia) of sponges.   Common.
5. Hindia parva, *Ulrich.*   Common.
6. An undescribed genus and species of sponge.   Rare.
7. Diplograptus putillus, *Hall.*   Common.
8. Monticulipora (fragments).   Rare.
9. Arabellites cornutus, *Hinde.*   Common.
10. Arabellites sp.   Common.
11. Eunicites sp.   Common.
12. Cyphaspis (fragment).   Rare.
13. Beyrichia chambersi, *S. A. Miller.*   Rare.
14. Leperditia sp.   Rare.
15. Leperditia sp.   Rare.

16. Zygospira modesta, *Saq.*   Common.
17. Orthis testudinaria, *Dalman.*   Rare.
18. Tellinomya obliqua, *Hall.*   Rare.
19. Cleidophorus fabula, *Hall.*   Rare.
20. Cyclora minuta, *Hall.*   Common.
21. Microceras inornatum, *Hall.*   Common.
22. Bellerophon sp.   Rare.
23. Theca parviuscula, *Hall.*   Common.
24. Conularia trentonensis, *Hall.*   Rare.

It will be noticed that the only common fossils are silicious sponges, graptolites, jaws of annelids, *Zygospira modesta,* and the minute forms of gastropods, pteropods, and lamellibranchs.   The Bellerophon, Conularia, and Theca represent pelagic types, and the remaining forms, not microscopic, are so sparsely distributed that they were probably transported specimens, or at least did not flourish where found.

The BRACHIOSPONGIA are in their natural position in the rock, and evidently were buried without having been removed from their original bed.   The presence of the numerous masses of filamentous spicules, or basalia, may be explained by their having originally grown in the soft mud of the sea bottom, and thus were protected, while the exposed cups of the sponges would be subject to dissolution and destruction unless previously covered.

CONDITION OF PRESERVATION.

The spicules of the dermal and gastral surfaces are usually replaced by calcite, and the parenchyma of the sponge is commonly filled with silica.   Previous to the process of mineralization, the spicules, pores, and interior canals, in many specimens, were enveloped in a thin film of peroxide of iron, and, although the invasion of silica and calcite has involved the entire space occupied by the organism, this film now serves to differentiate the various structures, so that a satisfactory study may be made of their leading features.   Many of the more minute and delicate spicular membranes are probably destroyed.

It has been shown by Dr. G. J. Hinde (Cat. Foss. Sponges, p. 7), that very few of the silicious sponges are preserved as fossils in their original condition, and that a replacement of the spicules by crystalline calcite is of very common occurrence. Even in a silicified fossil sponge, the silex is not in its original state, but has been altered or replaced by silica of a different condition.

The majority of the specimens of BRACHIOSPONGIA in the collections have been weathered out of the rock, and are represented as silicified casts. Owing to the usual exemption of the dermalia from silicification, the superficial structures are not preserved in weathered examples, nor in specimens which have been freed with acids. The exposed surface of these casts shows merely the extent of the process in the parenchyma, and the inequalities in its distribution. In rare cases, the dermal skeleton has been silicified, and its features obliterated, except the large hypodermal pentacts, which are represented by numerous papillæ on the surface.

The first alteration of the original colloid silica of the sponge was, apparently, to calcite, which also filled many of the interior canals, and, with few exceptions, destroyed the axial canals of the spicules. The subsequent invasion of the silica and partial solution of the calcite have, in some instances, separated and enclosed the calc rhombs, and such specimens when weathered now exhibit rhombic cavities in the silica. Ordinarily, however, the calcite has been simply replaced by silex in the form of chalcedony, except in some of the larger cavities which are incrusted with quartz crystals.

In order to preserve and study the dermalia and gastralia, it is necessary to secure specimens more or less enveloped in the matrix, and to uncover them with instruments. The limiting structures may be further exposed by the use of caustic potash, which removes much of the argillaceous limestone filling the pores.

SYSTEMATIC POSITION.

CLASS SPONGIA.

Order HEXACTINELLIDA, O. Schmidt.
Suborder LYSSACINA, Zittel.

Family BRACHIOSPONGIDÆ, nobis.

Dermalia forming a quadrate mesh, in which are immersed large free pentacts, or modified hexacts. Parenchyma thick, with large free hexacts, and more or less cylindrical canals, the outer ends of which are covered with the dermal mesh.

Including the genera,

> BRACHIOSPONGIA, Marsh.
> STROBILOSPONGIA, nobis.

Genus BRACHIOSPONGIA, Marsh, 1867.

(Am. Jour. Sci., 2d Ser., Vol. XLIV, p. 88.)
[Type *Scyphia digitata*, D. D. Owen.]

Sponge in the form of a broad cup or vase, with a row of projecting processes or arms around the periphery of the base, and into which the gastral cavity is extended. Osculum large, not operculate. Afferent and efferent canal system well developed.

Dermal skeleton composed of a fine network of spicules, in which are immersed large pentacts with the proximal rays penetrating the parenchyma. Gastralia large and free. The observed parenchymalia consist of hexacts which are sometimes variously modified. Supported on the sea bottom by the peripheral arms and broad base; not anchored by bundles of spicules.

4

STROBILOSPONGIA, gen. nov.

[From the resemblance to the "Strobila" stage of Aurelia, and from the twisted base.]
[Type *Strobilospongia tuberosa*, nobis.]

Sponge cyathiform or globose, with more or less concentric rows of lobes or lobed expansions, on the surface. Anchored to the sea bottom by means of massive bundles of filamentous spicules (basalia) proceeding from the interior of the base of the cup. The bundle of basalia is well defined at its origin, and does not merge into the tissues of the sponge. The spicular structure of the parenchyma, so far as observed, agrees with BRACHIOSPONGIA. Both the known species show numerous cruciform spicules on the surface, but they are so obscured by silicification that their detailed form and relations cannot be ascertained. Smaller spicules and traces of a continuous dermal mesh are also imperfectly indicated.

Any systematic division of paleozoic sponges into orders and families is necessarily incomplete and unsatisfactory. The structures are but partially, and often not at all preserved, and, therefore, the data for a settled classification are to a large degree wanting. It is, however, of importance to give the geological distribution of the paleozoic Hexactinellida, and this is done in the table on page 16. With it is introduced a grouping of the genera, which has in part been advanced by previous writers.

The family Euretidæ, into which many of these forms were originally placed, has since been restricted by Schulze and von Lendenfeld to genera agreeing more closely with Eurete. The family Pollakidæ is probably not a natural one, and it is now a convenient receptacle for genera of doubtful affinities.

Hydnoceras (= Dictyophyton, *Hall*) and allied genera are well characterized by transverse and longitudinal bundles of long rayed spicules, which divide the surface into squares generally arranged in fours, and by the absence, so far as known, of a fused dictyodermal layer. The parenchyma is also comparatively thin. Professor James Hall has proposed the family Dictyospongidæ to include genera possessing these features. The group appears to be a well-founded and natural one, and belongs to the suborder Lyssacina. In addition, Astylospongia was removed from the Hexactinellida, by Zittel, in 1884,[1] so that it is now significant that no paleozoic sponges are known, which can with certainty be referred to the suborder Dictyonina.

This fact may have an important bearing upon the phylogeny of the suborders. As stated by Schulze, either the Dictyonine forms have been derived from the Lyssacine by fusion of the spicules, or both suborders have been derived from a primitive form by gradual and parallel division. At present, all the known paleozoic hexactinellids appear to belong to the Lyssacina. The suborder is represented by numerous and diverse species, and seems to have reached its maximum development previous to the appearance of true Dictyonina.

There are several genera of fossils in the earliest formations, which have as yet yielded but scant evidences as to their proper relations. Among these may be mentioned the genera Calathium, *Billings* ; Trachyum, *Billings* ; Spirocyathus, *Hinde* ; and Trichospongia, *Billings*.

A summary of the distribution of the genera as presented in the following table shows that the rocks of the Cambrian (Taconic) system have furnished two genera which have not been found in any of the succeeding formations. From the Silurian, twelve genera are recorded, seven of which are peculiar to the system, while four pass into the Devonian, and one of these continues into the Carboniferous. The Devonian has afforded but one genus peculiar to it, and the other four cited are found also in earlier or later formations.

---

[1] Neues Jahrbuch für Mineralogie, etc., 1884, Bd. ii, pp. 75–80, Taf. i, ii.

Distribution of Paleozoic Hexactinellida.

Suborder Lyssacina, Zittel.	Cambrian. (Taconic.)	Silurian.	Devonian.	Carboniferous.
Family Dictyospongidæ, Hall.				
Protospongia, *Salter*	—	.	.	.
Cyathophycus, *Walcott*	.	—	.	.
Hydnoceras, *Conrad*	.	—	■	—
Ectenodictya, *Hall*	.	.	.	—
Plectoderma, *Hinde*	.	—	.	.
Lyrodictya, *Hall*	.	.	.	—
Thamnodictya, *Hall*	.	.	.	—
Phragmodictya, *Hall*	.	.	.	—
Cleodictya, *Hall*	.	.	.	—
Physospongia, *Hall*	.	.	.	—
Uphantænia, *Vanuxem*	.	.	—	.
Family Brachiospongidæ, Beecher.				
Brachiospongia, *Marsh*	.	—	.	.
Strobilospongia, *Beecher*	.	—	.	.
Family Pollakidæ, Marshall.				
Hyalostelia, *Zittel*	.	?	.	—
Holasterella, *Carter*	.	.	.	—
Leptomites, *Walcott*	—	.	.	.
Astroconia, *Sollas*	.	—	.	.
Amphispongia, *Salter*	.	—	.	.
Acanthinella, *Hinde*	.	.	.	—
Family Monakidæ, Marshall.				
Astræospongia, *Roemer*	.	—	—	
Family Receptaculitidæ, Hinde.				
Receptaculites, *De France*	.	■	—	.
Ischadites, *Murchison*	.	■	—	.
Acanthoconia, *Hinde*	.	—	.	.
	2	12	5	10

Variety and habitat of the Paleozoic Hexactinellida.

In a review of the paleozoic hexactinellid fauna, more than twenty genera must be considered, all of which probably belong to the suborder Lyssacina. The diversity of form and degree of specialization in these ancient sponges seem to be even greater than is exhibited among the recent species. From such simple cup-shaped forms as Protospongia and Cyathophycus, there is a regular gradation to the angular and nodose Hydnoceras, with the closely allied genera Lyrodictya, Cleodictya, Physospongia and others belonging to the family Dictyospongidæ, including, also, the wonderful basket disk of Uphantænia. Hyalostelia represents the enormous root spicules of an otherwise unknown form. Astræospongia has the form of a compact concavo-convex disk. Brachiospongia with its fingered cup, and the elaborate Strobilospongia with its solid bundles of anchor spicules, and, finally, the Receptaculites, with no recent representatives either in form or structure, exhibit the wonderful development of the Hexactinellida during paleozoic time.

Altogether, the facts point to the culmination of the Lyssacina at this period.

The recent Hexactinellida are characteristic deep-sea types, ranging from a depth of ninety-five fathoms to abyssal regions. In a study of the paleozoic forms, it is interesting and important to determine, if possible, the conditions under which these sponges flourished. Deep sea investigation tends to show that the present abyssal oceanic areas and continental masses are of great antiquity, and, consequently, that we can have but limited areas and localized horizons representing deposition below the 100-fathom line. Also, it has been shown that detrital sedimentation almost ceases below 100 fathoms, and any organisms found in such formations must have lived in areas of less depth.

The evidence furnished by observations on many of the paleozoic hexactinellids shows that although occurring in groups of strata often containing an abundant fauna, yet the particular beds, or layers, preserving the sponges in their greatest perfection and abundance are comparatively barren of other organisms. In some cases, they must have thickly covered the sea bottom. The *Hydnoceras tuberosum* from Steuben County, N. Y., occurs in countless numbers, at several limited horizons, in a fine grained and at times argillaceous sandstone. It is rarely associated with specimens of crinoids and brachiopods. *Hydnoceras prismaticum* occurs under similar conditions. *Cyathophycus reticulatus* is found also in great numbers on the slabs of Utica Slate, from Holland Patent, N. Y. In BRACHIOSPONGIA, it is shown that the associated fossils include pelagic species and others not incompatible with a deep water habitat. Rarely are other organisms associated with these sponges, although the conditions were evidently such as would have preserved them. The occurrence, too, of these delicate lace sponges in so great abundance and in an unbroken state shows that the waters were tranquil, and that they were removed from active physical changes.

It seems reasonable to suppose that the most characteristic and permanent of the deep sea types were among the first to remove from the littoral zone, and that they were the earliest to develop features adapted to a deep sea existence. In many organisms, the retention of brilliant colors and mineral characters common among littoral forms shows that they have migrated from the shores to a deep water habitat without developing into perfect harmony with the environment, and that they are comparatively recent additions to the deep water fauna.

On the contrary, many of the deep sea genera have lost their littoral features, together with many morphological and chromatic specializations, and are in accord with their surroundings. Hence, the species within the present limits of these genera are strictly a development under deep water conditions, and to-day have no littoral representatives. Only in remote time, or ancient deposits, are related or ancestral forms found, exhibiting a shallow water distribution.

The recent hexactinellid and lithistid sponges are among the most extensive groups which are peculiar to the deeper zones. Their abundance and great development in the Cretaceous are in accordance with other faunal and lithological features, indicating the deep water origin of that formation From this, it is probable that, at an early period, these orders flourished in the deeper regions of littoral deposits, and at greater depths.

While there is no strong reason for considering the deposits containing Brachiospongia as having been formed in very deep water, yet they cannot well be considered as belonging to a littoral fauna.

Description of Species.

Brachiospongia digitata, Owen.

Plate I, figs. 1, 2 ; Pl. II, figs. 1–7 ; Pl. III, figs. 1, 2 ; Pl. IV, figs. 1–5.

Sponge broad cup-shaped, or short vasiform, with a row of arms (from eight to twelve observed) projecting outwards and downwards from the periphery of the base. Osculum elliptical, with the diameters usually in the ratio of two to three. Below the osculum, the walls of the cup, or neck, are vertical, extending for a distance of from 25 to 40 mm., and slightly expanding below to the origin of the arms.

Fig. 1.

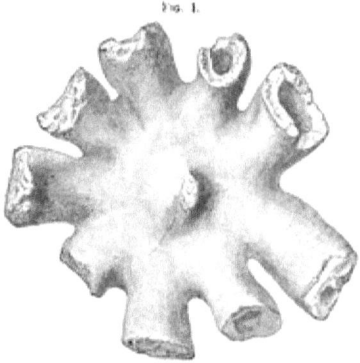

Figure 1.—*Brachiospongia digitata:* base of the original specimen. One-half natural size

Base of cup concave, usually with a strong conical or mammiform projection near the center, which is the initial point of the sponge (fig. 1). The gastral side of the base at the initial point shows several pits, of which from three to five have been seen (Pl. II, fig. 7).

The arms are distant from each other from one-fourth to one-fifth their diameter at the base. Starting from the origin of the arms, they are nearly circular in transverse section, and extend outward at right angles to the sponge axis, or frequently upwards, and then are abruptly bent downwards, flattened along their outer faces, and terminate in a compressed extremity which is rarely bifid. When in a perfect condition, the arms are closed at their distal ends.

The increase in the size of the arms is not altogether commensurate with the growth of the sponge, and to compensate for the separation of the arms, new ones are added from time to time. Plate I, figure 2, shows a wide space on one side of the longest arm, and as this is about the maximum size for nine-armed specimens, further growth would have developed another arm at this point. A portion of a ten-armed specimen is shown in Plate II, figure 3, in which a new arm has just begun to start out from the cup, and now appears as a large node, or swelling, between the widely separated and divergent adjacent arms. A still farther brachial development is represented in figure 4 of the same plate. The specimen has eight normal arms besides the central one in the figure, which is about half grown. In the collections studied, comprising twenty-one nearly entire specimens, the number of rays varies, with some exceptions, according to the size of the individual, and is from eight to twelve. Further research will probably extend these limits.

In the following table, the grouping is based upon the number of arms. It shows the variation in size, and enumerates the specimens in each group.

Number of arms.	Diameter of smallest and largest specimens, in inches.	Number of specimens.
8	$9\frac{1}{4}$	1
9	$4\frac{3}{4}-6\frac{1}{4}$	4
10	$3\frac{1}{2}-9$	9
11	$5\frac{1}{4}-11$	1
12	$6-10\frac{1}{2}$	3

One of the individuals here indicated as having ten arms is $5\frac{1}{2}$ inches in diameter, and shows in addition to the ten fully developed rays, three nodes, and two branched arms, all spirally arranged, beginning at the initial point, and extending to the osculum of the sponge. A ten-rayed example, having a diameter of 6½ inches, presents ten normal arms, and one node representing an undeveloped arm (Pl. II, fig. 3).

The accompanying wood-cut, figure 2, illustrates an abnormal specimen, and shows very clearly that, for specific distinctions, little dependence can be placed upon the number and character of the arms. On one side of the specimen, they are normally developed, while, on the other, they are bifurcate and covered with processes and large rounded protuberances.

Fig. 2

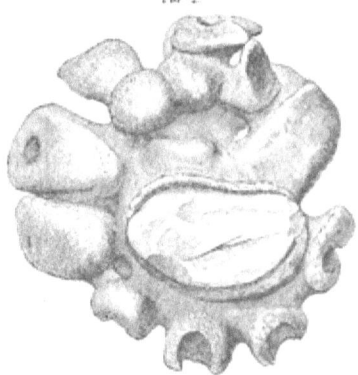

FIGURE 2.—*Brachiospongia digitata*; abnormal specimen. One-half natural size.

From what is shown regarding the growth and increase of the arms, it is evident that this feature is not of sufficient importance to be used as a basis for specific separation. With but two or three specimens at hand representing the extremes of variation, these differences seem to be important. Having numerous individuals, however, representing different stages and conditions of growth, we are able to connect the extremes, and, at the same time, show the wide extent of this mutable and mirable species.

The gastral cavity is very large, occupying the whole interior of the cup, and extending nearly to the distal extremities of the arms.

6

Some specimens which were freed from the rock without the use of
acids show that the extremities of several of the arms, and the basal boss,
were worn through to the gastral cavity before they were imbedded. But
the present imperfect condition of many of the weathered specimens is due
principally to breakage, and to the non-silicification of portions of the
sponge walls.

Dimensions.—The smallest example observed (Pl. II, figs. 5, 6, 7) has
nine arms, and measures 45 mm. in height. This is somewhat less than
the original height, as the neck is imperfect, and the extremities of the
arms broken off. The greatest diameter is 80 mm., and the arms have a
diameter of about 16 mm. at their bases. Two of the largest individuals,
preserving their full extent, measure about 275 and 330 mm. respectively,
in diameter.

A restoration from fragments in the collection, based upon the proportions presented by entire specimens, indicates that the largest individuals
of this species reached a diameter of about 400 mm.

BRACHIOSPONGIA is among the largest of the fossil Hexactinellida, and
ranks in this respect with Uphantænia and Cleodictya, although they are
all somewhat exceeded by the recent genera Pheronema and Poliopogon.

It is interesting to note that in the cavities of BRACHIOSPONGIA and in
the surrounding rock are numerous small spherical bodies which suggest
the statement made by Schulze,[1] that in the cavities of *Poliopogon amadou*,
were small spherical sponges about 3 mm. in diameter, which he considered
as the young of that species. In the present instance, however, these
bodies vary in size from 1.5 to 10 mm., and show a structure which is
characteristic of Hindia, and the species has been named *Hindia parva*, by
Mr. E. O. Ulrich.

A specimen of BRACHIOSPONGIA (Plate III, fig. 1), found by W. M.
Linney in the northern part of Spencer County, Kentucky, in strata of the
Middle Hudson series, offers some points of difference with those from
Franklin County. It is preserved in mudstone, and the parenchyma of the
sponge has been replaced by calcite. The specimen measures 255 mm.

---

[1] Rep. on the Hexactinellida, p. 237.

in diameter, and has eight arms, which are constricted at their origin, directed outwards and downwards at an angle of forty-five degrees, and are not geniculated as in typical *B. digitata*. The osculum is subcircular, and the neck is campanulate below. The cup, or body, of the sponge is comparatively small. The base is flat, and without the initial projection usually present. Were it not for the great range of variation shown in the specimens from Franklin County, it would seem that this form represented a distinct species. The differences are probably due to changed physical conditions.

Spicular Skeleton.—Rod-like spicules were detected in the matrix adjacent to the dermalia, in some of the sections made for microscopic study. They were without apparent regularity, and probably correspond to the uncinates or raphides in the dermal membranes of many recent forms. As their relations are uncertain, they have been omitted in the diagrammatic restoration given in Plate IV, figure 8.

The surface of the sponge when well preserved presents a minutely papillose appearance to the unassisted eye. The papillæ are of unequal size, irregularly arranged, and distant 1 mm., or less. When magnified, they are seen to be produced by an elevation of the dermal membrane, and by five strong conical nodes occupying the center. It is shown that the latter belong to large free hypodermal pentacts.

The dermal membrane (Pl. IV, fig. 1) is composed of an exceedingly fine and irregular quadrate mesh of four-rayed spicules, apparently fused, with their centers distant from each other from .1 to .2 mm. Occasionally, larger spicules occur, which seem, with the expansion of the surface due to the growth of the sponge, to develop eventually into the large pentacts of the hypoderm.

The hypodermalia are less regularly arranged than the dermalia, and the rays overlap and cross each other in various directions. The proximal rays have been observed to penetrate the parenchyma to the depth of 2.5 mm., and the tangential rays reach a length of more than 1 mm.

The parenchyma varies in thickness with the size of the specimen, and in different portions of the same individual. It is thinnest near the extremities of the arms and at the edge of the cup. A specimen 80 mm. in greatest diameter has a parenchymal thickness of 3 mm. near the ends of the arms and edge of the cup, and reaches a thickness of nearly 5 mm. near the origin of the arms. The walls in the central portion of an arm 52 mm. in diameter are 10 mm. in thickness laterally, and somewhat thinner on the distal and proximal sides. A large arm nearly 60 mm. in transverse diameter shows a thickness of 13 mm.

The accompanying wood-cuts (figures 3 and 4) represent actual sections through two arms, and show the thickness of the parenchyma, the irregular canals, and the diameter of the gastral cavity, in each. The lower edge is the flattened outer face of the arm.

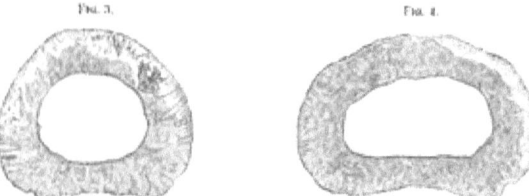

Fig. 3.   Fig. 4.

Fig. 3.—*Brachiospongia digitata*: section across middle of arm.
Fig. 4.—*B. digitata*: section across lower third of arm, from larger specimen.
Both figures are natural size.

The parenchymalia seem to be all hexacts, exhibiting great variations in size and in the development of the rays. Many of them are of about the size of the hypodermalia, but much larger occur. Their principal axes are usually parallel or vertical to the adjacent surface of the sponge, and frequently one or more rays are greatly developed, and seem to bear spines or lateral processes. In one broken section, a single ray may be traced for a distance of 10 mm. Other weathered specimens show many similar elongate rays traversing the parenchyma. In rare instances, the axial canals are preserved, and appear to have been about one-third the diameter of the rays.

No evidence is shown on the exterior of the sponge of the presence of the interior canals or afferent pores, but on the gastral surface of the walls are numerous oscula between the rays of the spicules, often radially arranged, and with larger circular depressed areas 2 to 3 mm. in diameter marking the terminations of the principal efferent canals. The interior, represented in horizontal section, in figures 3 and 4 of Plate IV, exhibits irregular cavities filled with crystalline quartz, and cylindrical vertical canals having a diameter of from 1 to 2 mm. The gastral ends of the large canals are covered with a membrane in which no spicules can be detected. It is perforated by several efferent apertures, or oscula. Also, the walls of the entire canal system appear to have had a limiting membrane, probably spicular originally, but now preserved as rusty markings in the rock.

The gastral membrane does not seem to be as well preserved as the dermal, nor are the spicules so well differentiated. It is covered with a layer of pentacts which are irregularly disposed, and not fused into a connected mesh. The largest pentacts measure about 2 mm. across, and interspersed with them are numerous smaller spicules. The proximal rays of the larger pentacts extend into the parenchyma, as represented in Plate IV, figure 7.

Summary of spicular and internal characters.—Dermalia constituting a continuous, minute, irregular, quadrate mesh of four-rayed spicules. Hypodermalia consisting of larger immersed pentacts with an elevated exsert node at the base of each tangential ray, and a similar central node representing the atrophied distal ray; proximal ray penetrating the parenchyma.

Parenchymalia comprising large and small hexacts with modified rays, which are sometimes spiniferous. Gastral membrane with numerous, irregularly arranged, large and small pentacts and tetracts, which are apparently free; proximal rays long, penetrating the tissues. Dermal pores not defined; gastral pores irregularly circular or oval, sometimes disposed in a radial arrangement. Gastral surface marked by circular depressions covered by a perforated membrane, and marking the terminations of the main interior efferent canals. Parenchyma penetrated by numerous irregular canals and by vertical cylindrical canals.

Geographical Distribution.—The specimen found by Dr. Troost is recorded as from Davidson County, Tennessee. Others have been collected in Mercer and Spencer Counties, Kentucky. The most prolific localities known are in Franklin County, Ky., on Benson Creek and its tributaries, northwest of Frankfort, and on Cedar Run, two and one-half miles south.

STROMBOSPONGIA TUBEROSA, sp. nov.

Plate V, fig. 8 ; Plate VI, figs. 3–7.

The form of the sponge is somewhat conical, flattened, and deeply indented longitudinally on opposite sides, from the base to the osculum. Otherwise, the surface is covered with slightly pendent, solid, tuberose extensions of the parenchyma. Summit flattened.

Osculum irregular, sinuous; margin thin, sometimes convoluted. Base broad, giving a truncate appearance to the cup: penetrated by a large mass of basalia, or root tuft of anchor spicules, extending into the interior nearly one-half the height of the parenchymal portion of the sponge. In one example, the bundle of anchoring spicules, where it emerges from the base, has a diameter of more than one-third that of the body of the sponge above.

The principal specimen (Pl. VI, figs. 3, 4, 5) has a height without the root tufts of nearly 80 mm., and the greatest diameter across the base is 110 mm. It is remarkable as preserving a bud which is still attached to the parent mass, and nearly equals it in size. The root of the bud is a little smaller, and the lobation of the surface is considerably sharper and more distinct. A smaller individual 70 mm. high is very irregularly formed. One side is lobed as in the preceding example, and the other is marked by two deep irregular pits. A vertical section was made through this example revealing the extent of the mass of basalia and of the gastral cavity. It is represented in Plate VI, figure 6.

The specimens are so thoroughly silicified that the spicular structure has been to a large degree obliterated. The cruciform ends of large hexactinellid spicules can be seen on some portions of the surface, resembling those in similarly preserved specimens of *Brachiospongia digitata.*

Smaller dermal spicules and traces of a spicular mesh can likewise be detected. The parenchymal canals are nearly vertical to the surface, and measure .6 mm. in diameter. The basalia are closely aggregated, and usually form a twisted rope-like bundle. The separate spicules are very slender, not measuring more than .02 mm. in diameter. The axial canals are occasionally preserved, and are represented in Plate VI, figure 2.

The source of the two specimens of the species here described is quite uncertain. They were received accompanied by labels referring them to the Hudson group, from Turner's Station, in northern Kentucky. The condition of preservation and enclosing matrix bear much resemblance to some specimens of BRACHIOSPONGIA, whose location is known. The presence, too, of another species of the same genus, and of so many similar masses of basalia in the Brachiospongo bed, serve to point to this horizon as the probable source of the species.

On Plate V, figs. 2, 3, 4, three masses of basalia are shown, representing their general features. The microscopic structure is delineated in Plate V, fig. 5, a, b, and Plate VI, figs. 1, 2. Ropes of spicules, both larger and smaller than those illustrated, were collected. One example has a diameter of 110 mm., and others measure that number of millimeters in length. These numerous root tufts indicate imperfectly the richness of the original sponge fauna represented in these sediments. In an area of not more than two square rods, on Cedar Run, about forty specimens were obtained on the surface of the ground. They are also common near Bridgeport, Franklin County, and at several places on Benson Creek.

Similar masses of basalia have been called Tricholites, but it is obvious that several slightly related forms of sponges may have anchoring bundles of spicules, which are undistinguishable from each other, and that specific, or even generic characters are seldom impressed on the root tufts. The genera Leptomites, Hyalostelia, and Acestra, represent varieties of basalia for which the sponge proper has not been discovered. Recently, root spicules were described for the genus Protospongia, by Sir Wm. Dawson and Dr. Geo. J. Hinde,[1] but they do not form a massive bundle.

[1] Canadian Record of Science, Montreal, April, 1888.

Distribution.—The two specimens of *S. tuberosa* bear the label "Turner's Station, Ky." Numerous masses of basalia have been found in and above the Brachiosponge bed on Benson Creek, Cedar Run, at Frankfort, Franklin County, and at Lexington, Fayette County, Kentucky. Under the name *Tricholites typicalis*, Mr. E. O. Ulrich has catalogued similar bundles of spicules from the tops of the hills at Cincinnati, Ohio.

STROBILOSPONGIA AURITA, sp. nov.

Plate V, fig. 1.

The only example of this species known is a compressed cup-shaped specimen found associated with BRACHIOSPONGIA, on Benson Creek. The summit and base are both imperfect, and the special features of these portions cannot be described. There is a flattened, depressed area down the center of the sides, which is without ornamentation. The specimen preserves five concentric imbricating rows of auriculate pendent extensions of the parenchyma, some of which are so closely appressed to the cup that the underlying tissues are excavated for their reception. In general, these expansions appear to be solid, but several show that the gastral cavity extends into them for a short distance.

The microscopic structure is no better preserved than in the preceding species, and the spicular skeletons of both agree in all the features which can be observed.

The specimen has a height of 156 mm., and a maximum diameter through the center of 138 mm. The latter dimension is somewhat greater than normal, on account of the compressed condition of the sponge. It is completely silicified, and preserved in a condition similar to the majority of the specimens of BRACHIOSPONGIA.

As compared with *S. tuberosa*, this species reaches a greater size and is more robust, the parenchymal expansions are much larger, pointed directly downwards, and more regularly arranged in concentric rows.

Distribution.—From the Brachiosponge bed on Benson Creek, Franklin County, Kentucky.

PLATE I.

PLATE I.

BRACHIOSPONGIA DIGITATA.

Page 19.

FIG. 1.—Original specimen; lateral view. *Natural size.*

FIG. 2.—The same; seen from above. *Natural size.* *Davidson County, Tenn.*

Original in Yale University Museum.

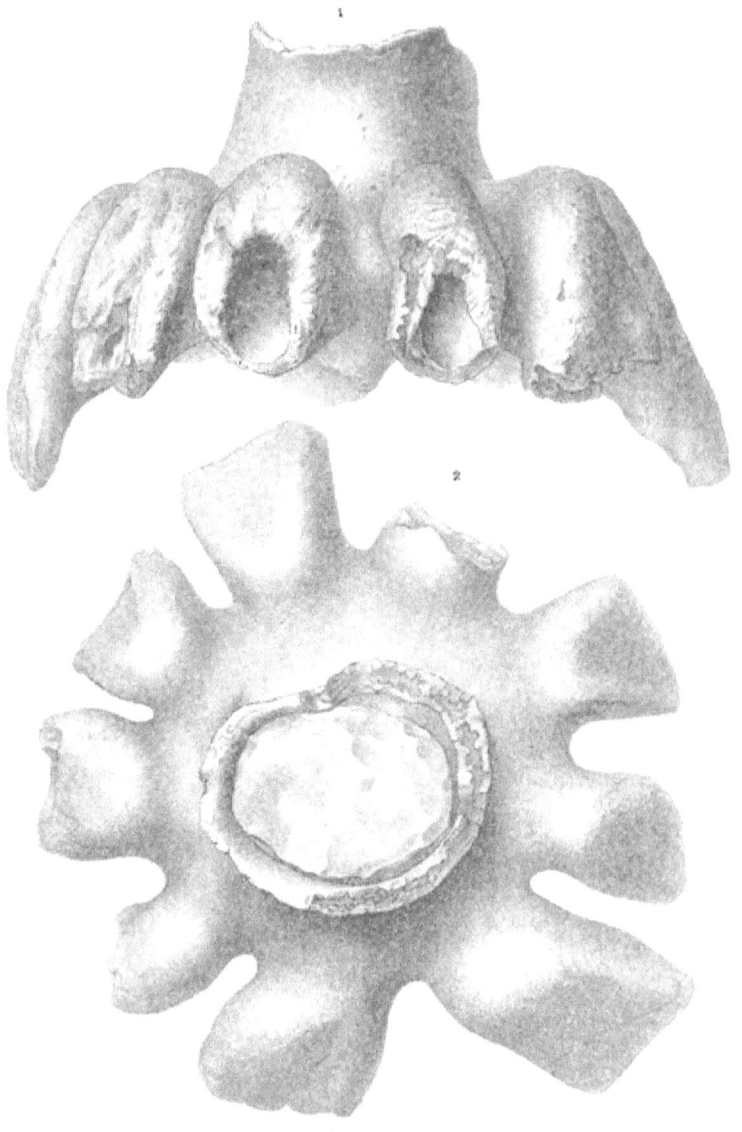

PLATE II.

PLATE II.

BRACHIOSPONGIA DIGITATA.

Page 40.

FIG. 1.—Side view ; showing full extent of arms.

FIG. 2.—The same ; showing section through cup, and openings into gastral cavities of arms. *Natural size.*

FIG. 3.—Side view of imperfect specimen ; showing initial point in growth of one arm, which here appears as a swelling, or node. *One-half natural size.*

FIG. 4.—Another specimen ; exhibiting one arm apparently about half grown. *One-half natural size.*

FIGS. 5, 6, 7.—Lateral, bottom, and top views of smallest specimen observed. *Natural size.*

Brachiosponge bed. *Franklin County, Ky.*

Originals in Yale University Museum.

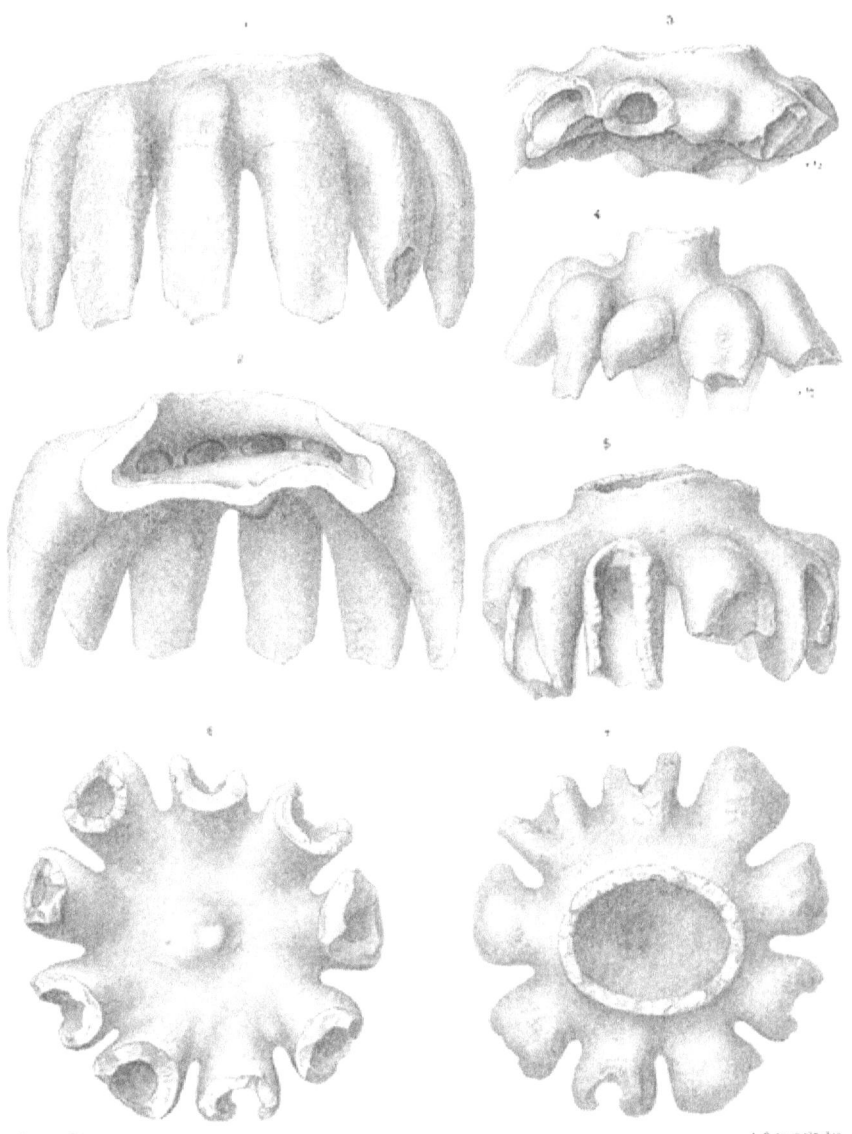

PLATE III.

PLATE III.

BRACHIOSPONGIA DIGITATA.

Page 40.

FIG. 1.—Top view of eight-armed specimen mentioned on page 22. The parenchyma has been partially exfoliated, and the cast of the interior is exposed in several places. *One-half natural size*. Middle Hudson. *Spencer County, Ky.*

FIG. 2.—Lower side of large twelve-armed specimen, in the collection at the State Museum, Frankfort, Ky. *One-half natural size*. Brachiosponge bed. *Franklin County, Ky.*

Original of figure 1 in Yale University Museum.

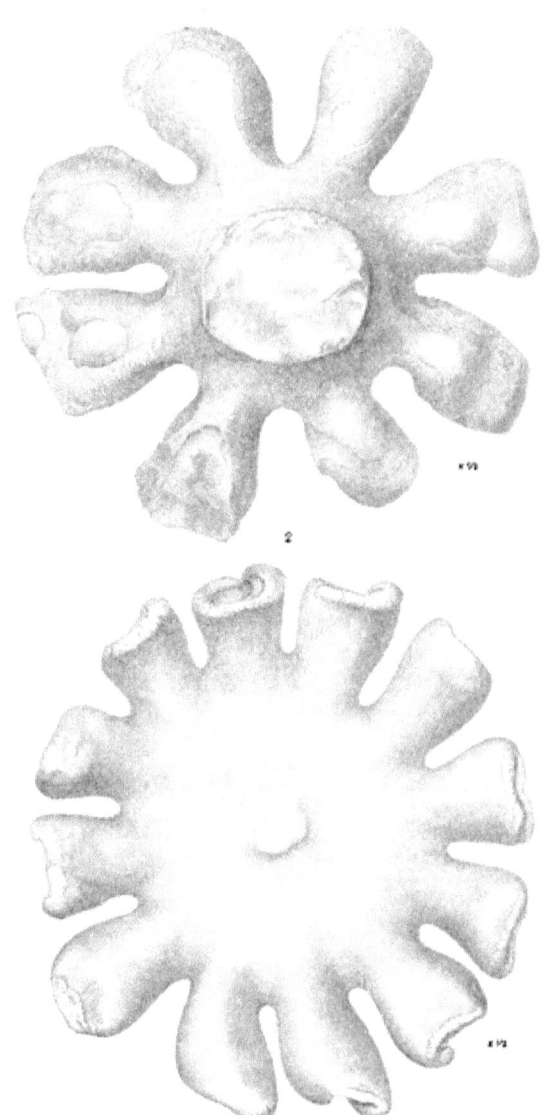

2

× 1/2

× 1/2

PLATE IV.

PLATE IV.

BRACHIOSPONGIA DIGITATA.

Page 28.

Fig. 1.—Outer surface of sponge; showing dermal spicular mesh and exsert nodes on rays of hypodermal pentacts. × 20.

Fig. 2.—Section representing large hypodermalia after removal of dermal mesh. × 20.

Fig. 3.—Horizontal section of interior of parenchyma. × 20.

Fig. 4.—Horizontal natural section from broken specimen. × 4.

Fig. 5.—Subgastral skeleton; showing large spicules and ends of efferent canal system. The circular depressions represent ends of vertical cylindrical canals. × 10.

Fig. 6.—Inner, or gastral, surface. × 20.

Fig. 7.—Vertical section through parenchyma with small portion of adhering matrix on dermal side. × 20.

Fig. 8.—Restored vertical section, combining characters represented in the preceding figures, which were drawn from actual specimens. × 10.

Originals in Yale University Museum.

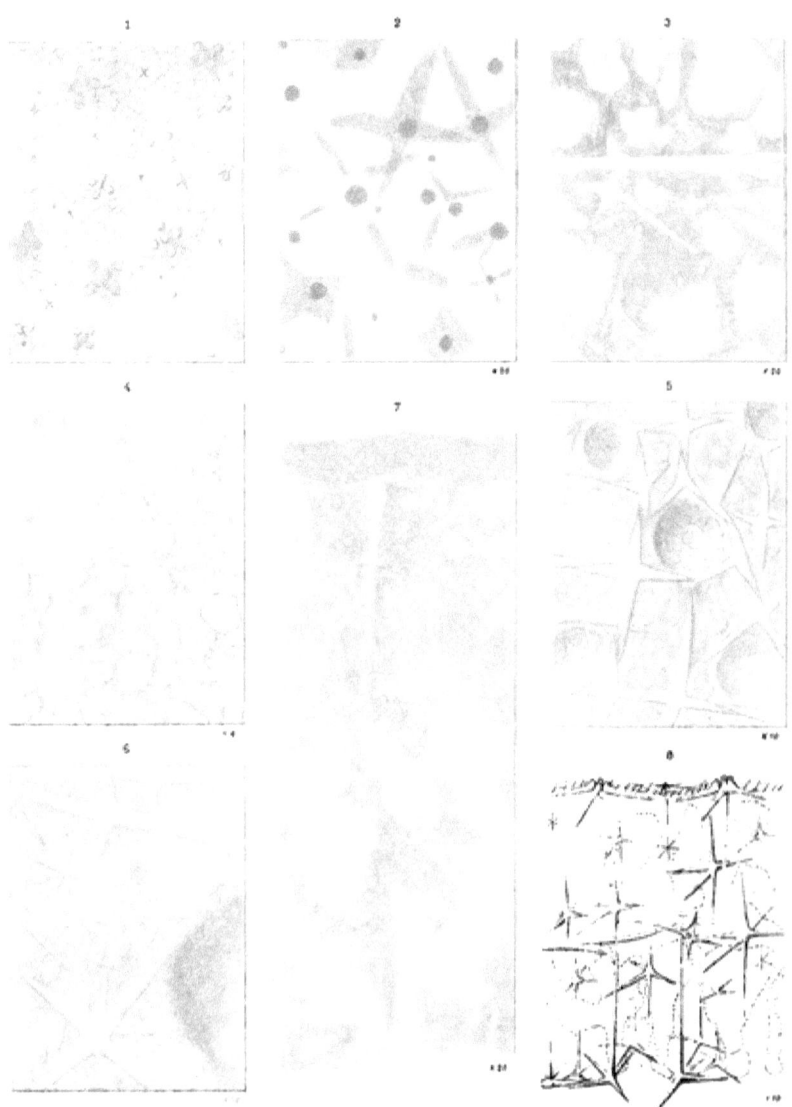

PLATE V.

10

PLATE V.

STROBILOSPONGIA AURITA.

Page 28.

Fig. 1.—Lateral view of type specimen. *Natural size*. Brachiospongc bed. *Franklin County, Ky.*

BASALIA.

Page 27.

Figs. 2, 3, 4.—Three masses of anchor spicules presenting characteristic features. *Natural size*. Brachiospongc bed. *Franklin County, Ky.*

Fig. 5.—*a*. Longitudinal section of small portion; showing size and disposition of basalia. × 25.

    b. Transverse section from same specimen. × 25.

    c. Section of small fragment of parenchyma of *Strobilospongia tuberosa*, showing two imperfectly preserved hexactinellid spicules. × 25.

Originals in Yale University Museum.

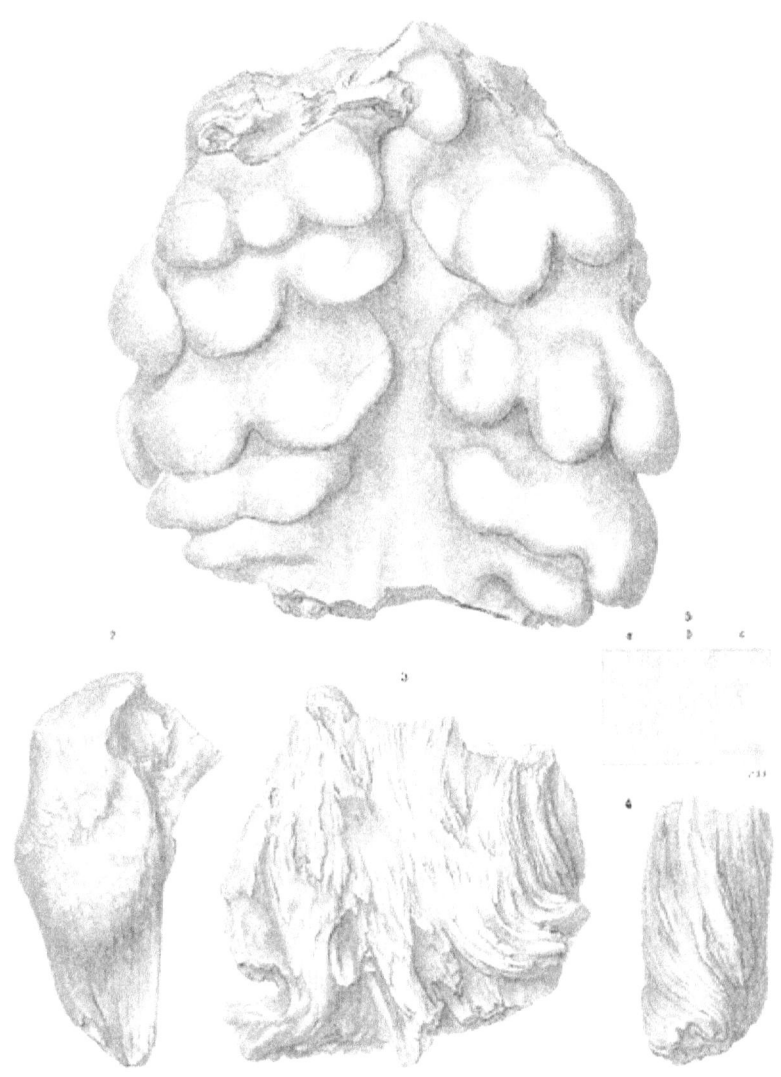

PLATE VI.

PLATE VI.

BASALIA.

Page 27.

Fig. 1.—Longitudinal section of fragment. × 70.

Fig. 2.—Transverse section; showing diameter of spicules and axial canals. × 70.
  Brachiospongia bed. *Franklin County, Ky.*

STROBILOSPONGIA TUBEROSA.

Page 26.

Fig. 3.—Lateral view; showing parent sponge at the right, and attached bud on the left
  with its separate bundle of basalia. *Natural size.*

Fig. 4.—Basal view of same specimen.

Fig. 5.—Side view of bud; showing strong lobation of surface.

Fig. 6.—Small example, cut longitudinally through the center; exhibiting extent of
  bundle of basalia, gastral cavity, and variable thickness of parenchyma.
  Natural size.

Fig. 7.—The same; showing external form of sponge, and narrow and sinuous aperture
  at summit.

  Both specimens of this species are recorded as from the Hudson group at
  Turner's Station, Ky.

  Originals in Yale University Museum.

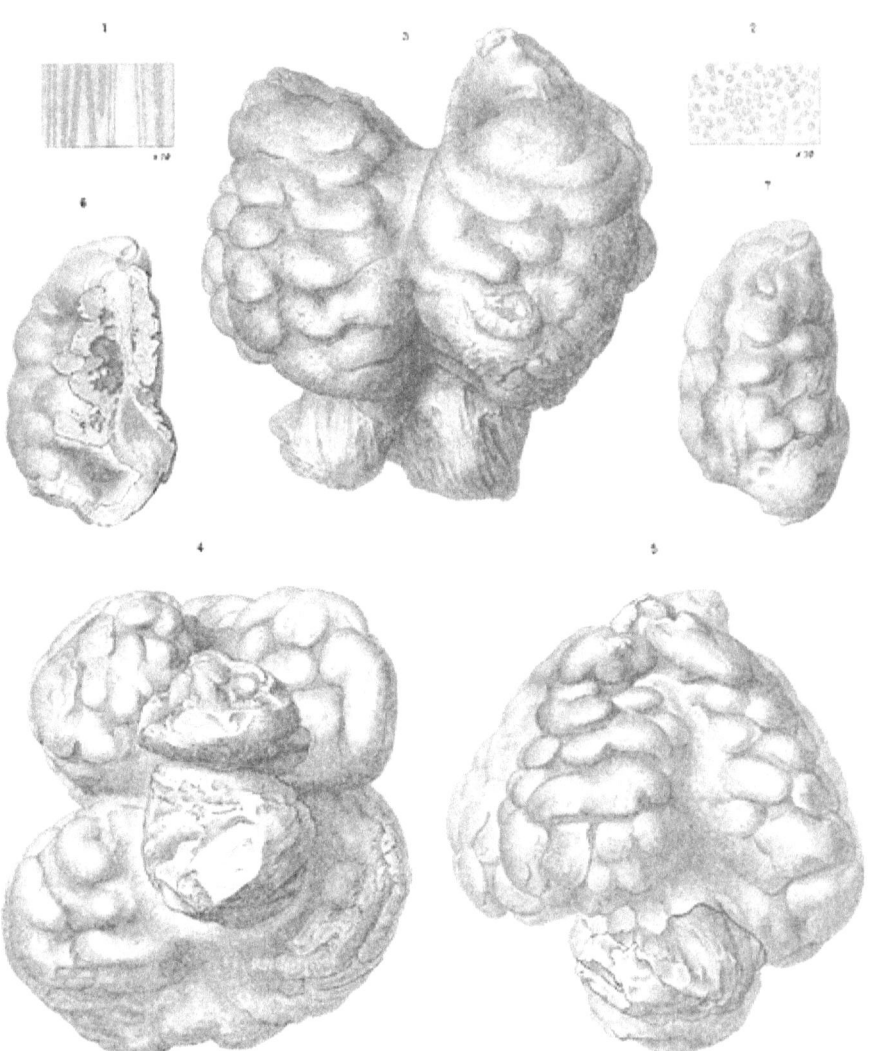